THE PRODIGAL CHILD

SELECTED WORKS BY
Irène Némirovsky

TRANSLATED FROM THE FRENCH BY SANDRA SMITH

Suite Française

David Golder

Fire in the Blood

Le Bal and *Snow in Autumn*

The Courilof Affair

All Our Worldly Goods

The Dogs and the Wolves

Jezebel

The Wine of Solitude

The Misunderstanding

The Fires of Autumn

THE PRODIGAL CHILD

Irène Némirovsky

Translated from the French by
Sandra Smith

KALES PRESS

Kenneth Kales, Editor
Bonnie Thompson, Associate Editor
Barbara J. Greenberg, Assistant Editor

Jacket design by Laura Klynstra
Book design by Jennifer Houle

Library of Congress Cataloging-in-Publication Data in process
Names: Némirovsky, Irène, 1903–1942, author. | Smith, Sandra, 1949–translator.
Title: The prodigal child / Irène Némirovsky ; translated from the French by
    Sandra Smith.
Other titles: Enfant génial. English (Smith)
Description: First edition. | San Diego, California : Kales Press, 2021. | Summary:
    "Following Irène Némirovsky's international bestseller Suite
    Française comes one of her earliest works: The Prodigal Child, a story of hope
    that turns into one of betrayal"—Provided by publisher.
Identifiers: LCCN 2021024319 (print) | LCCN 2021024320 (ebook) | ISBN
    9781733395847 (hardcover) | ISBN 9781733395854 (ebook)
Subjects: LCSH: Poets—Fiction. | Child authors—Fiction. | Jewish children—
    Fiction. | Inspiration—Fiction. | LCGFT: Fiction. | Novels.
Classification: LCC PQ2627.E4 E5413 2021 (print) | LCC PQ2627.E4 (ebook) |
    DDC 843/.912—dc23
LC record available at https://lccn.loc.gov/2021024319
LC ebook record available at https://lccn.loc.gov/2021024320

Printed in the United States of America

First Edition

ISBN-13: 978-1-7333958-4-7 print edition
ISBN-13: 978-1-7333958-5-4 ebook edition

kalespress.com
San Diego, California

It is not the luxury that you admire.
You imagine a perfect life in which everything
is order and beauty.

—Irène Némirovsky,

diary entry, 1920,

foreshadowing *The Prodigal Child*

INTRODUCTION

Irène Némirovsky was born in Kiev in 1903. Her father, Léon, was a wealthy banker, which was unusual at the time, as he was Jewish. His position allowed the family to enjoy a luxurious lifestyle, including a French governess for their daughter, as French was considered the language of the upper classes and diplomats at the time. Irène's first languages, therefore, were French and Russian, and all her works were written in French. At the beginning of the 1917 Revolution, the family was forced to flee, and after a few years in Scandinavia, they finally settled in Paris; Irène was sixteen. By then, she already spoke French, Russian, Finnish, and Swedish, as well as some English and German.

As an avid reader in many languages, Némirovsky was interested in different literary genres, something that is evident in this short novel. This work combines biblical parable with Greek mythology, fable, and elements of children's fairy tales and yet is set in what was then contemporary Russia. As in all these genres, our story has a moral—or, rather, many morals.

The Prodigal Child is one of Némirovsky's earliest works, written in 1923 (when she was only twenty years old) but not published until 1927. Its original title was *L'enfant génial* ("The Child Genius"), but the book was released in the Gallimard edition of 2006 as *Un enfant prodige* ("A Child Prodigy"). For this translation, I have chosen the title *The Prodigal Child* because of the overwhelming similarities between the biblical parable and the content of the novel. Némirovsky's titles always have a multitude of suggestive meanings in French, and it is often up to the translator and publisher to choose a title that best describes a work.

Our tale begins with a clear reference to the Bible; its first two words are "Ishmael Baruch," the name of the protagonist. The biblical Ishmael was the son of Abraham and his wife's handmaiden, Hagar, born when Abraham believed that his wife, Sarah, could not bear children. But many years later, when Sarah gave birth to Isaac, she insisted that Hagar and Ishmael be cast out. Ishmael is credited with being a prophet—if not the founder—of Islam, while Abraham, Sarah, and Isaac carried on the line of Judaism.

The protagonist's last name, Baruch, is the Hebrew word for "blessed," and most Hebrew prayers begin with *"Baruch atah Adonai"* ("Blessed are you, O God"). So the novel begins with a paradox: the protagonist is both blessed and cast out. This theme continues throughout the work.

Ishmael's "blessing" is his gift for composing poetry and songs—which is reminiscent of the Orpheus legend. His inspiration is completely natural, instinctive, and the novel thus deals with the concepts of creativity and inspiration as well:

> *Ishmael continued singing, and his heart grew*
> *lighter, lighter within his chest, like a bird about*
> *to take flight. And a strange clarity filled his*

mind, the kind of clarity that exhilaration or delirium sometimes brings. . . .

Never did the boy think about the words in advance: they came to life in him like mysterious birds to whom he only needed to give a little nudge, and the music that accompanied those words came just as naturally.

When people discover Ishmael's gift, his life changes completely. He meets a woman he calls "the Princess," which adds the fairy-tale element to the novel. It is a rags-to-riches story, as she is fabulously wealthy and negotiates with his parents to have the child live with her in her mansion; she then takes charge of his education, in order to cultivate his genius.

The paradoxical symbolism continues throughout this novel. Némirovsky shows us a mirror image of the traditional genres that she so cleverly intertwines. In the parable of the prodigal son, the boy leaves with all his wealth, squanders it, and returns poor but is welcomed back and honored by his father. In the Bible, his father is meant to represent God, who forgives sinners if they repent and return to the fold. In Némirovsky's tale, however, the child leaves poor, becomes fabulously wealthy—along with his parents—but is cast out by the Princess when he loses his gift, and his father is far from pleased.

Why does Ishmael lose his gift? Némirovsky offers several possible reasons in the text but leaves us to draw our own conclusions. Does spontaneity simply fade during the rite of passage that changes a boy into an adolescent? (Ishmael is only ten when the story begins and fifteen when it ends.) Is it his passionate attachment to and child-like love for the Princess? Or perhaps the reason lies in the discovery of the great classical authors he reads in the Princess's library:

> *He loved the Princess with all his heart, with the*
> *feverish, ardent little heart of a prodigal child.*
> *As for the books, they made him jealous and*
> *unhappy; unconsciously, he started imitating*
> *the verses of others. When that happened, a kind*
> *of hateful rage surged through him: his former*
> *songs seemed laughable to him, pitiful. And*

*short stories—he did not know why—seemed
even worse. Up until now, he had looked at
nature and people with his own eyes and translated what they meant to him very quietly
through his own words. But now, suddenly, the
distorting, perfidious mirror reflecting the soul
of other people slipped in between the outside
world and his own soul. . . .*

*There were poems that he couldn't speak out
loud without weeping, and others that filled him
with an emotion that was almost like terror.
And when he remembered his songs, they
seemed so pitiful, so awkward, so inept and
foolish that he felt infinitely ashamed, humiliated, and miserable.*

With passages such as these, Némirovsky poses questions that all artists ask themselves, and she unveils their
innermost fears: they question their own talent, they will
not compare favorably to others, the critics will use their
influence to make or break them:

Then, to his dismay, he read scholarly books
that analyzed the act of writing, all the complex
cogs in the mechanism of creation, and he was
like a man who, on the point of accomplishing
some insignificant gesture, would have to seek
out all the infinitesimal elements that make up
the will to act, and he would be left dazed, dis-
traught, facing the sheet of paper that remained
obstinately blank. But when he looked up and
saw the countryside stretched out before him, he
would flee far away from human knowledge.

One final issue we encounter when reading this short
novel is the representation of the Jews in the tale, an issue
that needs to be placed in context. Némirovsky's family
was an exception in Russia at the turn of the twentieth
century, when Jews were extremely limited in the profes-
sions they were allowed to practice, and most were very
poor. Many of her novels depict the terrible conditions of
the Jews living in the ghettos and the difficulties they
faced due to their religion, especially in France during
the 1930s, when anti-Semitism was rife. This novel is no

exception. In the very first paragraph, we learn that
Ishmael's family had lost everything during "a pogrom."
His grandfather is a moneylender; the Jews in the market
are expert at bartering. The Baruchs are extremely poor,
live in the ghetto, and have many children, who either die
or leave in search of a better life:

> [The] family grew larger every year, for chil-
> dren multiplied like insects in the Jewish
> quarter. They grew up in the streets. They
> begged, argued, swore at passers-by, rolled
> around half-naked in the mud, ate vegetable
> peelings, stole, threw rocks at dogs, fought, filled
> the street with an ungodly clamor that never
> ceased.

Nevertheless, many of Némirovsky's works stress the
importance of acknowledging or returning to one's roots,
and many of her Jewish characters face disaster when
they ignore that instinct and instead attempt to assimi-
late. Conversely, they find peace and hope when embrac-
ing their heritage.

To Ishmael as well, his Jewish roots are a positive influence and a source of inspiration:

> *Sometimes, he would tilt his head and begin*
> *slow, plaintive chants that these Slavs had*
> *never before heard, and that were simply an*
> *unconscious echo of the sad Jewish songs that*
> *arose from the depths of time like an immense*
> *sob, growing stronger and stronger through the*
> *ages, until they reached the child's soul.*

Sadly, Irène Némirovsky felt the brutal force of anti-Semitism during her brief lifetime. Never granted French citizenship, subject to the cruel laws against the Jews during the Nazi Occupation, which forbade her to be published, she was deported to Auschwitz in 1942 and murdered there at the age of thirty-nine. The same fate befell her husband, Michel Epstein, also a Russian Jew. Their two children, Élisabeth and Denise, survived; they escaped with a family friend and were hidden by teachers, nuns, and other Resistance workers until the end of the war.

We are fortunate that Denise Epstein discovered her mother's unfinished masterpiece, *Suite Française*, and agreed to have it published in France in 2004. It has since been translated into more than forty languages. This one novel brought Némirovsky recognition throughout the modern world as the great author she was and allowed all of her previously published novels and numerous short stories to be rediscovered.

I was privileged to get to know Denise and become her friend. We traveled together on many book tours, and I was honored to serve as her interpreter. At the launch of the English translation of *Suite Française* in London, the very first time we met, she was in her mid-seventies. I will never forget her opening words: "I couldn't accept my mother had died, until I could see her reborn."

In its lyricism, symbolism, mixing of genres and universal themes, *The Prodigal Child* bears all the marks of the important author Irène Némirovsky was to become.

Sandra Smith
New York, 2021

THE
PRODIGAL
CHILD

shmael Baruch was born on a very snowy day in March, in a large trading port on the Black Sea in southern Russia. His father lived in the Jewish part of town, not far from the Market Square, where he sold old clothes and scrap metal. He still wore a threadbare caftan, Oriental slippers, and the short side curls called *payos*,[1] as was ordained. His wife helped him with his work and bore his children. Over her hair, which had been shaved off on the day of her wedding, as commanded by the Law, she wore a curly black wool wig that made her look somewhat like a dark-complexioned woman whose skin had been bleached white by the rain and snow of the North. She was a hard worker, no more frugal than necessary, and well-mannered. She remembered the happier times of the past, for her father had been a rich moneylender before they burned down his house during a pogrom, on the Easter Sunday after the assassination of Emperor Alexander II.

---

[1] The side curls worn by Orthodox Jews that signify obedience and loyalty to God.—Trans.

The only thing Ishmael's mother had left from her former opulence was a pair of gold hoop earrings that were more precious to her than her sight itself. They jingled with a bright mocking sound as she came and went in her creased, stained dress made of printed cotton, cleaning the house, washing the floors on Friday, or cutting the black bread and cloves of garlic into very small pieces, which she would feed to her household.

Her family grew larger every year, for children multiplied like insects in the Jewish quarter. They grew up in the streets. They begged, argued, swore at passers-by, rolled around half-naked in the mud, ate vegetable peelings, stole, threw rocks at dogs, fought, filled the street with an ungodly clamor that never ceased.

The Baruchs had fourteen of them. As soon as they were old enough, they left for the port, where they did all sorts of odd jobs: they helped the longshoremen and porters, sold watermelons they'd stolen, begged for alms, and prospered like the rats that scurried around the old boats along the coast.

Once in the clutches of the town or the sea, such children rarely returned home; many of them left on the large ships loaded with cereal and grains, headed for Europe.

But most of them died young. Epidemics among the infants ripped through the Jewish quarter, sweeping away children by the hundreds. That is how the Baruchs lost half of theirs. One of their neighbors, a carpenter, would nail together a few boards as a coffin, in exchange for an old pair of trousers or a dented saucepan. The mother would weep a little, undressing the little body and laying it down in the new box that smelled of pine sap. Baruch would carry it under his arm to the Jewish cemetery, a sad, enclosed plot of land where graves without crosses lay close together, a place where flowers never grew. Soon another child would be born to replace the one who had died, wearing his clothes and taking his place in the corner of the old straw mat that served as a bed for the whole family. Then he would grow up and go away as well.

When Ishmael was about ten years old, he found himself alone. He noticed that his portion of bread and garlic had

Irène Némirovsky

gotten bigger. Then, one day, his father took him to the
Rabbi who taught the Jewish alphabet to the children of
that part of town. It cost one ruble a month, an amount
Baruch would never have spent from his meager budget
if he'd had other sons, or the hope of having more, but he
and his wife were getting older, and Ishmael was their
youngest.

Ishmael quickly learned to read, write, chant prayers, and
recite verses from the Bible by heart.

It was warm at the Rabbi's house, and in the winter,
Ishmael loved staying there for hours on end, snuggling
in the warmth of the wood-burning stove, while all
around him, some twenty little voices repeated a plaintive, monotonous, holy verse, without ever growing
weary. But when they wanted to teach him to count, he
ran off, wandering around the port as his older brothers
had before him.

The town was either baking hot in the summer sun or
freezing in the glacial winter winds, but in springtime,
the wild, free waves of the sea were infused with all the

scents of Asia. Ishmael loved the town and the port. He also loved the Market Square on summer mornings, with its heaps of tomatoes, peppers, melons, and the golden strings of onions twisted around the workbenches. The merchants opened the red bellies of the fish; the small green tart apples that the housewives used to make preserves marinated in buckets of salty water. Ishmael would collect *boubliks*[2] that passers-by dropped on the ground, or a handful of cherries half-crushed by horses. Watermelon peels were scattered all over the streets; there were barrows heaped with the ripe fruit, as heavy and round as green moons. People would cut them into sweet, red, juicy pieces; as soon as Ishmael had a kopek in his pocket, he would buy one, then spend the rest of the day sucking its rosy flesh, which melted in his mouth.

On the Market Square, you could see people of three different races who stood shoulder to shoulder but never mixed: Russians, with their long, dirty beards, kind eyes in simple faces, each with two or three large features that make them look like white wooden toys, their Orthodox

---

[2] Small Russian bread rolls shaped like a wheel.—Trans.

priests, with the long, straight hair of Christ, and peasants in cotton blouses, merchants in silk smocks. Then the Tartars, their heads wrapped in turbans, who never spoke much and were content to simply silently offer the buyers their trays full of nougat, Turkish delight, and Armenian incense. And, finally, the Jews, dressed in their grease-stained greatcoats, talkative, obsequious, hopping about like old birds, wading birds without feathers who understood everything, knew everything, sold everything, and bought even more.

And the sun streamed down over all these things, and the eternal sea breezes danced joyously in the dust, and when night fell, the bells from the Orthodox church rang out, calling, echoing, stifling the voice of the call to prayer from the rooftop of the only mosque, whose silent white silhouette softly faded into the night.

But more than all of them—Jews, Tartars, Russians— Ishmael preferred the unclassifiable riffraff that swarmed into the port, people from the Middle East who smelled of garlic, the tide, and spices, swept up by the sea from every corner of the world and thrust there like the foam on the waves.

They would sleep all day long in the shadow of the small fishing boats that rotted in the stagnant water of the port. But at night, they would meet in the nearby inns, to drink, fight, and, sometimes, sing in all the languages of all the countries of the world. Ishmael had made friends with several of them: sailors, porters, vagabonds. He helped them do their work, and in this way, he managed to earn his daily bread. When night fell, instead of going back to the shop, he would often follow them to the inn. These men enjoyed giving him drinks. By the age of ten, he had tasted all types of alcohol, imported from the four corners of the world: Russian vodka that tasted like fire, Turkish raki, gin, and other terrible concoctions, which he swallowed, grimacing horribly, but without complaining, proud of being admired.

Then his head would start to spin, the smoky walls of the tavern danced before his weary eyes, and through the sweet sleepiness that bound his arms and legs, the voices of the singers reached his ears, more mysterious and more intense.

A big lad named Sidorka, who had sailed the Volga for years on end before washing ashore on the Black Sea, taught Ishmael the songs they sang on the river. Ishmael soon knew them all by heart; he had a clear voice, both piercing and sweet at the same time, and he sang without ever growing weary, until he fell asleep, intoxicated as much by the music as by the eau-de-vie.

Sidorka lived with Lisanka, one of the sailors' whores; she was pretty but had a terrible scar on her right cheek that disfigured her. Sidorka beat her mercilessly and regularly took the little money she earned. One day, she suddenly died. Sidorka sold the meager goods she'd left behind and went to the inn, and after he'd been drinking, he started to cry.

This happened one summer night when it was very hot and the sky was full of shimmering stars. Sidorka left the stinking room and went to sit outside on the parapet. His legs dangled in the empty space, a liter of eau-de-vie at his side.

Ishmael followed him. In the darkness, you could hear the water from the port splashing about, and the nearby boats creaking. Ishmael touched the drunkard:

"Are you sad?"

The other man did not reply; he was swaying like a bear and very quietly humming a vague melody.

He finally said in a thick voice: "Sing for me, little one . . ."

"What would you like me to sing?" asked Ishmael.

"Sing for me, little one . . ." Sidorka said over and over again, without hearing him.

Ishmael straddled the parapet, beating his bare feet on the stone to keep time; he began singing the lament of the *burlaks*,[3] but the man stopped him.

---

[3] A *burlak* was a person who hauled barges and other vessels upstream. They were mainly criminals, outlaws, or serfs who had run away. The main areas of the *burlaks'* trade in the Russian Empire were the Volga River, from Moscow to Astrakhan.—Trans.

"No, no, sing to me about Lisanka, Lisanka . . ."

"You're drunk," said Ishmael.

But Sidorka, with the stubbornness of a drunkard, kept begging him. Then he started to cry: "I loved her. . . . She died . . ."

Ishmael closed his eyes and started to sing—or, rather, chant—in a slow, pure voice that echoed in the silence of the night:

> *"She died, and I, I drag myself through the point-less day*
>
> *Like a fisherman drags his empty nets behind him, far away."*

"Yes, yes, that's it," Sidorka sobbed. "Keep singing, little one."

They were both swaying over the parapet, heads thrown back toward the immense sky, where the stars shimmered so brightly that they seemed to be sending a kind of sweet, endless echo to the entire firmament.

And Ishmael kept singing, intoxicated by the words he was inventing:

> *"She has died, the woman I loved more than my life itself . . ."*

He strove to chant the words using the phrasing of popular songs, now and again calling out a sonorous, guttural *"alas!"* that Sidorka would repeat in his powerful voice. A few men came out of the inn; they surrounded Ishmael in silence. The music worked like wine on all those coarse, dazed men; they listened, astonished by the new song.

Ishmael continued singing, and his heart grew lighter, lighter within his chest, like a bird about to take flight. And a strange clarity filled his mind, the kind of clarity that exhilaration or delirium sometimes brings.

All night long, they had him sing; they joined in to sing the refrains that Ishmael discovered in his soul, like treasures placed there by God, for all eternity. When he stopped, exhausted, they poured him a drink. He finally fell silent and rolled off the parapet and onto the sand without hurting himself and fell asleep there among the vegetable peelings and shards of glass from the broken bottles.

ა

The next night, at the inn, they hoisted him up onto the table and had him sing again. Never did the boy think about the words in advance: they came to life in him like mysterious birds to whom he only needed to give a little nudge, and the music that accompanied those words came just as naturally. The fights, the shouting, the wild laughter of the drunken women did not bother him, for he continually invented drinking songs, and all the noise and clamor were indispensable to them. Sometimes, he would tilt his head and begin slow, plaintive chants that these Slavs had never before heard, and that were simply an unconscious echo of the sad Jewish songs that arose from the depths of time like an immense sob, growing stronger and stronger through the ages, until they reached the child's soul. Then everyone would fall silent, form a circle around him, huddling together to better hear him, enchanted, their bright eyes wistful in their brutish faces.

They made him sing the same thing twenty times; he indulged them willingly, proud of his superiority over these men, who could have easily destroyed him with a single blow, prouder than Orpheus must have been as a child when he played to the wild beasts. His fame resounded throughout the area. He was a young Jew, hardened by his fate, so he asked for money every evening. Handfuls of kopeks were thrown at him; soon he didn't need to do any other kind of work. During the day, he slept in the sun or wandered the streets; the other children his age treated him with deference, for he had the protection of all the rabble of the port. At home, however, his reputation impressed no one—at least, not yet. Realizing that Ishmael had stopped going to school, his father scolded him, and his mother lamented. But since Ishmael was bringing home money, they let him be. He made only brief appearances at his father's shop; he felt suffocated by its damp darkness. Such resigned mediocrity was unbearable to him: he preferred the poverty of his sailor friends, who at least never wanted for alcohol, music, or women.

Little by little, the Baruchs began to think of Ishmael as lost to them, just like his thirteen brothers and sisters, who had gone far away or died. And used to suffering, they were resigned to adding this grievance to all the others that the Lord seemed pleased to inflict on them and their race.

Now, for three evenings, a man had joined the sailors in the Bout-du-Quai inn and had listened to Ishmael. It was winter, and the icy winds from the Russian steppes danced in gusts around the closed ports. The man wore an otter coat and a fur hat that came down to his eyes. The regulars there did not know him, and the owner looked askance at him at first. But one night, he paid for everyone's drinks, and the next day, he left fifty rubles as payment for two bottles of vodka that cost thirty-five kopeks each. After he'd gone, everyone whispered that he was a Barine,[4] and one of the girls, Machoutka, claimed to know him and to have seen him in certain unsavory places along the port. He was a prince, she said, generous and rich, and he liked drinking and frequenting brothels and inns. That did not surprise them much: the officers and lords of the area often ended up in the port's *traktirs*[5] at night, but in groups, never alone, unlike the Barine, whose countenance commanded respect, but with no one to defend him from all the nasty young boys. He would arrive, sit down without saying a word, and methodically get drunk. Then his eyes would light up; the most charming of smiles would endlessly illuminate his thin, ravaged face. He would pay for drinks, dance with the young women, then leave after having given money away to everyone who believed in God, as Sidorka put it.

One evening, after Ishmael had stopped singing, the Barine called him over with a vague gesture of the hand: "Come here, little one . . ."Ishmael stood in front of the

---

[4] This was a title given to a member of the Russian nobility at the time.—Trans.

[5] Inns, usually with restaurants.—Trans.

stranger and let him look him up and down. The Barine was definitely drunk, but in his bloodshot eyes, there was a kind of clear admiration that was unknown to Ishmael. He reached out toward the boy's curly mass of hair with long, slim fingers that trembled slightly due to the alcohol.

"What's your name?"

"Ishmael."

"You're Jewish?"

"Yes."

"Where did you learn your songs?"

"Nowhere . . . I make them up . . ."

"Who taught you how to translate what you think and feel that way?"

"No one. . . . All the things I say are singing within me . . ."

A surprised look swept across the Barine's face, but he said nothing. He called the owner over, and simply pointed at his empty bottle. Once he had a fresh one, he turned toward Ishmael:

"Sing, little one. . . . I'm so sad . . ."

Ishmael had often heard such words, or similar ones, for all his friends from the port came to him when they were sad. He was quite familiar with the heavy, nebulous anguish that weighed on these simple souls whenever a bit of leisure time allowed them to vaguely think about their harsh lives, the injustice of their fates, their poverty, and death. Ishmael easily created songs from their sadness, the way primitive jewelry is created out of crude gold. But the Barine's melancholy puzzled him. His large eyes, full of distress and dreams, stared at the boy, spoke a language he could not understand.

The Barine waited. Ishmael lowered his eyes and, suddenly, asked: "Why are you so sad?"

"It's true, you can't know. . . . She's gone . . ." he said, smiling sadly. "Sing for me, and for her, little poet. . . . She's left me . . ."

The boy picked up a balalaika that had been left on a table; he'd learned how to play it a little. Then he began in a hesitant voice that grew more confident the longer he sang:

> *My beloved has left me, and I am so sad;*
> *Sing, drink, my friends;*
> *Your voices will chase away the dark*
> *demon of pain;*
> *The wine will drown my sorrow again.*

Every now and then, Ishmael plucked the strings of the balalaika with one hand; he sang with all his soul, as he had never sung before: a new, unfamiliar feeling of pride pierced his heart.

The Barine listened, his head in his hands. When Ishmael fell silent, he remained that way for a long time, without speaking, without moving. Then he raised his head,

absentmindedly rummaged through his pockets, and
threw money out in front of him, pieces of gold and
banknotes. Then he left, stumbling toward the door.
Ishmael could see he was crying. Around the table, there
was a terrible free-for-all; they were fighting over the
money the Barine had left. Candles were knocked over,
everyone was shouting, swearing; it was a battle. Women
screamed like crushed dogs; there was the dull thud of a
body falling. When the candles were lit again, all the
money had disappeared. Everyone suspected his neigh-
bor, but the thief was Ishmael, who had slipped between
the legs of the warriors, as agile as a cat, and had then
run off with the bounty. He ran as fast as he could
through the deserted streets of the port. Large clumps of
soft, wet snow stung his face; his bare feet were frozen
solid in his loose little boots—they were too big on him
and kept falling off with every step he took. But he felt
such extreme pride, such strange elation, that his arms
and legs were lifted, without him even caring where he
was going. And as he ran—blindly, quickly, confidently—
he truly felt he was being carried on the powerful wings
of a god. He didn't stop until he'd reached the parapet
along the quayside. At his feet, the sea unleashed its wild,

free waves. The little boy raised his arms in a great *hey!* of triumph, then rushed off again. His pockets were full of money; songs were born on his lips like the winter winds on the waves: he had made the Barine cry. . . . *Hey!*

For many long months, the Barine did not return. Ishmael continued leading his strange life. He was almost thirteen; he was tall and handsome, and behind a small, rotting boat, or in the shadow of a wall, women had already obligingly taught him how to make love. Afterward, they liked to listen to him sing, but as they sighed, feeling tender after his caresses, he would hum a mocking refrain and run off with the cruel laughter of a young man.

Now one night in December, they heard the little bells of the sleighs and the shouts of coachmen outside the inn; a group of drunken officers and noblemen flooded into the place. Ishmael recognized the Barine, who was with them; he was speaking very loudly and gesturing. His dilated pupils looked enormous in his face, reddened by the cold and alcohol.

Ishmael had been sleeping against the wood-burning stove when they came in.

He sat up straight when he heard the Barine shouting:

"Is the Jewish boy here? The little poet?"

Then, noticing the boy, he walked over to him.

"Come, over here. . . . Follow us. . . . You'll have as much money as you like. . . . But you have to stay with us all night, and sing your most beautiful songs for us. . . . She's come back, you see? My beauty, my queen. . . . Come on, come, come quickly, please, quickly . . ."

Pushed and shoved, Ishmael found himself outside, without quite knowing how, wrapped in a bearskin blanket and thrown like some package into the back of a sleigh. Then he heard calls, laughter, the cracking of the whip, and the long whistling of the wind in his ears, and the distinctive sound of the sleigh's sharp blades rushing through the hardened snow. He didn't move,

nestled in the fur, eyes wide open in the darkness, seeing nothing but a yellow lantern that danced before
him and lit up the horses' hindquarters, which were
covered in snow. They'd left the town and were racing
along—ten or fifteen carriages, one following another—
rushing through the countryside. Ishmael looked
behind him; he saw two shadows merged into one, kissing each other full on the lips. Looking at them more
closely, he recognized the Barine and saw a woman
dressed in black, wearing a large diamond around her
neck that sparkled eerily in the night. Then, snuggling up
under the fur cover against the legs of the man and
woman, who continued their embrace, he fell asleep,
enchanted.

ᖇ ᒷ

But not for long. He could feel someone carrying him, and
soon found himself standing in the middle of a large
room full of people. Later on, he learned that this house
outside the town was part of the famous "Black Village,"
where the gypsies lived. One by one, the sleighs stopped

in front of the steps, and drunken men came out shouting, singing, laughing. Their boots, full of snow, creaked on the marble floor of the entrance hall. Ishmael watched as dark-haired women, decorated with veils and sequins, rushed to meet them. Then they opened a door in front of him and pushed him into another room, a very small one with large divans, lit candelabras, a fiery wood-burning stove, and a table set for two.

In awe, Ishmael noticed roses in vases, and others in the folds of the tablecloth; his eyes grew wide with admiration: it was the first time in his life he'd seen flowers in December.

The Barine entered, holding the woman in black tightly to him. He led her to a divan and sat down beside her; then, as if ravenous, he began covering her hands and face with kisses. In the room next door, the others were sitting at tables, making an infernal racket. From time to time, they could hear a glass shattering noisily against a wall; the wild laughter of the drunken women seemed to pierce Ishmael's ears.

But the Barine's woman did not look intoxicated; her eyes were clear, mocking and perceptive. She noticed Ishmael standing, motionless, near the stove.

"The child must be hungry," she said.

"Of course, of course . . ." the Barine muttered. "Let him go to the kitchen, and—"

"But why?" she asked, cutting in. "Let him dine with us."

"If you'd like. . . . Your wish is my command, as you well know . . ."

Ishmael moved toward them, took the seat they pointed to, and began to eat. Never had he tasted such delicacies, but what attracted him the most was the champagne. The woman was now sprawled over her companion's knees, watching Ishmael through half-closed eyes. When he reached for the bottle of champagne, she gestured for him to stop:

"Don't . . . that's bad for children . . ."

He put the bottle back on the table with a look of surprise.

She smiled slightly.

"Go and open the door now, and tell the gypsies to come in."

Two men and a dozen or so dark-haired young women entered. The women were covered in jewelry and wore long veils that covered their faces. The singing and dancing began.

Ishmael stretched completely out on the carpet and, his heart pounding, listened to the poems that resembled his own, and the heathen music that has no equal anywhere in the world. The gypsies stood up, one after the other, and danced, undulating their unrestrained bodies beneath their veils. Then they whirled round and round, faster, ever faster, as the spectators clapped their hands, louder, ever louder, and everything seemed to spin around Ishmael in a wild, impudent, frenetic circle.

Suddenly, he felt the woman in black touch his arm:

"Does this please you?"

Moved by a kind of singular bravado, he shrugged his shoulders.

"My songs are far more beautiful," he replied. "And they will be for you, for you alone, Princess. . . . Afterward, no one will ever hear them again . . ."

"Very well," she said softly, "sing then . . ."

"Tell them all to leave and have someone bring me a balalaika, Princess."

"Why do you call me that?"

"Aren't you one?" he asked naïvely.

"No," she said, smiling again, "but that doesn't matter . . ."

She gestured for the gypsies to stop and leave her. They left in a commotion, emptying their glasses as they toasted her health. Someone gave Ishmael a balalaika, and he sat down on the floor, legs crossed in front of him, leaning against the wood-burning stove. The Princess, her cheek resting on one hand, watched him, absent-mindedly caressing her lover's hair with the other hand; he was sitting at her feet, kissing her knees through her dress.

Ishmael raised his strange, pale, anxious face toward them, hesitated for a moment, then began to sing. His words were simple and naïve, the same sorts of words that had so perfectly translated the pain and joy of the vagabonds of the port, and because of that, they stirred strange feelings in people's hearts. They had no rhyme, no cadence, just a natural rhythm, like the wind and the sea, a powerful and mysterious harmony.

The child sang in a pure, soft voice; his eyes stared out into the distance, seeming to follow a score visible only to him. The biblical adolescents brought to life by the breath of God must have resembled Ishmael.

When he'd finished, he looked at the Princess with simple and profound pride.

She remained silent.

"Little one," she said when she finally spoke, "you know that one day you will be a great poet, don't you?"

Then she added, as if to herself: "A prodigy, this little one . . . yes . . ."

He said nothing. What could he have said? He didn't know what the word meant.

The Barine sat up, resting on one elbow. "This child . . ." he said in the dreamy voice of a drunkard, "this child . . . didn't I promise you?"

"He can't remain the way he is," the Princess cried, "look at him . . . he's poor, ignorant, starving . . . a little Jew from the port . . . and yet, there is genius within him. . . . Don't you see?"

The Barine lazily reached for the bottle of vodka.

"He's happy the way he is . . ." he said. "He's happy because he doesn't understand his genius. . . . The day he does, he will be miserable. . . . I too was once a great poet . . ."

"And now you're just a drunkard, I know," she added harshly. Then she turned to Ishmael and questioned him with a kind of bitterness: "Little one, don't you want to be a great poet one day, rich and famous?"

"I don't know," murmured Ishmael.

An immense feeling of anguish rushed through him, fear and revolt against this woman who wanted to impose her will on his freedom.

But she stared at him with her dark eyes, as round as the eyes of a bird of prey, and said: "Would you like to live with me?"

Then, lowering his head, he replied: "Yes."

In the morning, a luxurious sleigh took Ishmael back home. His father, who hadn't seen him for three days, thought he would die of shock. Learning what had happened, he shook his head several times without saying a word and went out, telling his wife not to let Ishmael leave before he got back. Then he rushed out to see his father-in-law, the moneylender, who was a man who gave good advice.

Ishmael was hardly thinking of running away again; he was simply exhausted. He crept to a corner of the room, covered himself with his father's greatcoat, and fell asleep with visions of gypsies, feasts, and women dressed in black, diamonds at their necks, who danced around him with the silent laughter of witches.

Meanwhile, Baruch was getting information about the Princess. He quickly learned she was the widow of the former governor-general of the town. He also learned she owned a great deal of land in the South, including refineries and forests that covered several thousands of acres.

Lastly, he was told the name of her lover, the poet Romain Nord, and Baruch had no trouble in recognizing him as the one Ishmael naïvely called "the Barine." Nord had been living with her for six years. She would leave him and take him back again at her whim. To forget her, he drank, but that terrible vice did not save him: he claimed that at the bottom of his glass, through the wine, he could see the imperious face of his mistress, as if in a mirror.

After rushing through the entire Jewish quarter, Baruch went back home. The Princess was waiting for him in his shop. She was wearing perfume and was dressed in black furs, a small, dark hat covered her hair; its wings looked like a nighthawk's.

The Princess expected to be greeted as a good fairy godmother, but, to her great surprise, she was met with unexpected resistance; she was one of those haughty creatures who can bend destiny itself to her whims, the way you tame a wild horse to a saddle, but she had never before dealt with an old Jew from the Place du Marché. When she left Baruch's shop, after an hour of bartering, she realized she had promised them a small fortune for the right to be responsible for Ishmael's education and training. But she didn't understand that she'd been duped until everything had been agreed upon and the heavy waxed paper had been signed. It was too late to withdraw, and besides, she deemed this extraordinary little poet, with his crop of curly hair that fell nearly to his fiery eyes, worth everything she had to pay, and even more.

It was with truly great pleasure that she arranged the room that Ishmael would have as his own the next day.

The Princess lived in an ancient mansion at the end of a garden full of statues: scattered among the dark trees, a marble shape would emerge, smiling, with dead eyes, and the snow, like duck down, would form a white covering over it, emphasizing the pure outline of its beautiful, bare arms and legs.

The next day, a silent and serious Ishmael walked through the estate and the rooms of the mansion; they were decorated with tapestries and mirrors painted with birds and flowers in the Italian style. The Princess, enthralled, saw that he was very much at ease among all these things, things that, to him, were more extraordinary than visions of paradise. And when he'd been bathed, had his hair styled, and been dressed like a little lord in a velvet suit with a large pointed lace collar, he suddenly resembled a portrait by Van Dyck, a graceful child with long curls. He very quickly adapted to his new life, to which he brought the curious and precious skill of assimilation of his age and race, as well as a unique attraction to anything that was beautiful, rare, of noble heritage, or with harmonious colors. A special sense of instinct seemed to warn him of what he should say, what he should do, which words he'd learned in the Jewish quarter should not be repeated, what the Princess's gestures meant, while dining or in other circumstances of life, and, on the other hand, which were befitting to imitate. It was easy to him, for he was gifted with a priceless flair for spontaneity, normally only found in very young children.

The Princess was eager to take charge of his education. A former teacher from the senior school came every day to give him lessons; he learned quickly and well, with a kind of feverish thirst and a special, avid look deep in his immense eyes. Only one thing surprised the Princess: she had put many books in Ishmael's room—novels, travel books, and especially poetry—but she noticed that Ishmael rarely opened them. He even seemed to feel a kind of repugnance toward them, though he had learned how to read both Russian and Hebrew a long time ago, thanks to the conscientiousness of the Rabbi in the Jewish quarter. On the other hand, he spent endless hours clinging to the Princess's skirt while she played the piano or sang, and tears, round heavy tears, often slowly fell down his pale, enraptured face when he looked up at her.

He loved the Princess with all his heart, with the feverish, ardent little heart of a prodigal child. As for the books, they made him jealous and unhappy; unconsciously, he started imitating the verses of others. When that happened, a kind of hateful rage surged through him: his former songs seemed laughable to him, pitiful. And short stories—he did not know why—seemed even worse. Up until now, he had looked at nature and people with his own eyes and translated what they meant to him very quietly through his own words. But now, suddenly, the distorting, perfidious mirror reflecting the soul of other people slipped in between the outside world and his own soul. When he was near the Princess, however, all of that disappeared. Her eyes, her mouth were the sources of his songs, eternally renewing, like the sea had been in the past. . . . He had abandoned the sea a long time ago, content to simply look at it from afar, from the top of the austere quayside, lined with beautiful houses, which he passed in a carriage. The sea very calmly unfurled its waves at the end of a fine, sandy beach, dotted with pink seashells. One day, however, he wanted to see it again, up close, in the port, where its waves licked the rotting boats like a growling, affectionate dog. But as soon as he got to the ramparts, he was repulsed by the smells he'd forgotten, of the mud and rotting fish; even the Jewish quarter seemed small to him, full of poverty, noise, and stench. His parents, meanwhile, had moved. They now lived on one of the most beautiful streets in the city. Baruch was in business with his father-in-law, the elderly Salomon. He now shaved and wore a bowler hat and gold jewelry; Madame Baruch wore a silver ring with a diamond the size of a nut, even if the diamond was rather yellow in color. She no longer did the housework: a servant took care of that. She sewed all day long, like a lady, sitting by the window, and saw to the accounts.

Ishmael went to see them two or three times a week. Even the Messiah—if he'd deigned to descend to their house—would not have been received with so much love and respect. They were proud to have this opulent child as a son: well cared for, elegant, rich, and handsome, one whose prodigious future seemed so assured.

Meanwhile, Ishmael's life sped by with the strange rapidity of a dream. During the day, he learned, read, went horseback riding, and took long walks. In the evening, he accompanied the Princess and Romain Nord on their wild sleigh rides through the countryside. They quarreled in front of him or were loving to each other, depending on the day.

They often stopped at the "Black Village" and went into the hidden house surrounded by pine trees, a place where Ishmael had gone, one night, when he was a poor little vagabond. He now was very familiar with the long, flat road between two white plains, the entrance with its wooden steps, the sitting rooms that were too well heated, the lamps with their red shades that cast a deep, rosy shadow over the room, like the shadow that plays through your fingers when you hold them up to the light. He casually ate the finest dishes, used his knife and fork without fear, and the flowers that were always there, in winter as in summer, no longer caused him to marvel. He would absentmindedly cut off a rose, an expensive masterpiece that came directly from a wonderful land of eternal sunshine, wrapped in straw and tissue paper, and pin it on the lapel of his velvet suit. He knew the names of all the dark-haired women in their full, black dresses, their multicolored shawls, a red handkerchief tied around their heads; they sang in deep, coarse voices that grew suddenly sweet every now and then. Often they danced, their necklaces, bracelets, and crescent-shaped gold earrings making a tinkling sound as they clinked against each other. Ishmael would watch them, lying on the ground at the feet of the Princess. When it was his turn to sing, accompanying himself on the balalaika or guitar, the women would kneel down in a circle around him, like serpents listening to a snake charmer. When he saw their attentive, shining dark eyes, their small heads decorated with rows of sequins leaning in toward him, the smiles on their lips stained with wine, he would feel a unique sense of exultation rush through him that was translated into joyful songs that took flight, into lyrics that crashed and rang out like drumbeats. But when the women left, steeped in alcohol and money, Ishmael would sing for the Princess and the Barine: sad songs that made him want to cry himself, slow, long chants, as simple and painful as the music of the rain, the wind, the sea.

Then the Princess would reach out her long, pale fingers to touch his curls, full of caresses, and she would smile her surprising smile that lit up her entire imperious face before slowly fading away, leaving a slight quiver at the corners of her mouth, like a glimmer of light.

The Barine, his head in his hands, listened. He would drink some more and softly sigh, "I'm bored," staring out into the distance, as if sharing a secret, a plea, like the vagabonds of the port who also found no words to describe their sorrow. Then he would cry, and his tears would fall into his glass and be lost in the bubbles of the champagne.

Both of them would say, "Little poet . . . a child prodigy, a marvel . . ."

At other times, above his head, their eyes would meet, hazy with sudden desire; then, without a word, their lips would join for a long time. They kissed each other that way in front of Ishmael, without shame or fear, as if in the presence of the ivory Eros, dusted with gold, they had in their bedroom. And they did not see that the child grew thinner and paler with each passing day. They did not notice his drawn features, the dark rings under his sunken, burning eyes, his hot hands with their heavy fingers: he seemed to breathe in their passionate love as if it were a poisonous flower.

The Princess often organized celebrations at home in the grand white salon; she would sit Ishmael on top of a heavy malachite table, and he would sing, accompanying himself very sweetly on the balalaika or a lyre with a single string that the Princess had taught him to play. Ishmael sang without paying any attention to the men in their embroidered tunics, the women covered in jewels, wearing their most elegant evening dresses, who applauded him enthusiastically; he saw only the Princess. He stared at the sinuous lines of her mouth, which slowly opened in a smile of satisfaction and pride.

When he had finished singing, he was cajoled, embraced; the women sat him on their knees, pressed him to their breasts, swept their perfumed fingers, heavy with rings, through his hair.

And more than the terrible alcohol he had drunk in the past in the sailors' dives, this subtle intoxication was dangerous to him, for he was already a man, and beneath their dresses, he could imagine the shapes of the luxurious, beautiful bodies, and that filled him with slow, exquisite torture. It was said that he was handsome; he was flattered like some precious bauble, like a rare flower, and the pleasure he enjoyed from all the words spoken in front of him were, given his sensitivity, almost painful, like certain caresses that are too tender.

In a corner, there was a large armchair that Ishmael was particularly fond of; it sat in the shadows next to a pink marble vase, delicate and graceful, with bas-reliefs of dancing nymphs and masks of satyrs decorating its handles. He leaned back against the cushions and studied the ball as if it were a painting. Silk scarves and lace swirled past his eyes like clouds do when the north wind rushes over the plains. A vague but powerful scent of perfume rose from all the gathered women, as if from a bouquet of roses. A delightful feeling of vertigo gently filled Ishmael; he often fell asleep that way, dozing, interrupted now and then by subtle dreams, his warm cheek resting against the smooth, cool marble vase.

Then the women would disappear, one by one, carried away by tall officers in greatcoats with a thousand folds, as vast as hooped skirts. Sabers dragged along the paving stones of the entrance hall; the little bells of the sleighs rang softly in the sleepy town.

The valets had just extinguished the candles in the chandeliers; the darkened room seemed immense and full of mystery; the white walls shimmered in the moonlight; the open piano glowed dimly in the shadows. The string of a violin left outside its case, caressed by a gust of wind, vibrated slightly, as if sighing. A fan that had been

forgotten still had the scent of the ball in its feathers, min-
gling with the pervasive hint of dead flowers. In the
silence, a resonance of fading music hovered still, and in
their watery reflection, the misty mirrors seemed to echo
the flash of smiles on the faces leaning in toward them.

The Princess walked over to Ishmael, kissed him on the
forehead, and said good night. He pressed himself
against her without a word, yearning with a troubling
and subtle sensuality, and in the Princess's wide, somewhat mocking, melancholy eyes, an ineffable expression
would suddenly appear.

Once, when she was holding him that way, holding him
tightly against her, a large diamond set amid the reddish
lace of her bodice scratched Ishmael's cheek. The child
closed his eyes, nearly fainting at the slight wound, and
went completely pale.

Surprised, the Princess gently lifted his dark head; she
saw the blood that flowed from the little cut.

"Have I hurt you, Ishmael?"

"No," he said, violently shaking his long curls, "no . . ."

She started to move away. He threw himself against her, clutching her in an awkward, passionate embrace, and began rubbing his wounded cheek against the hard diamond, as if he had gone mad. But she only laughed very quietly, placed both hands around the child's upturned head, and, with an imperious expression, stared deep into his immense eyes, which blinked and closed, as if he were looking at a light that was far too bright. And she kissed him on the lips, wickedly, tenderly, the way you bite into the pink flesh of fruit.

Then she disappeared behind the folds of the blue velvet curtains.

෬৯

Every morning at eight, a servant came to wake Ishmael, who would go riding with the Princess from nine until ten o'clock, before his daily Russian grammar lesson. One day, when Piotr went into the child's bedroom, he saw his young master sitting on the bed, nightshirt open, hair disheveled, his eyes enormous and burning in his feverish, contorted little face. Overcome with fear, the servant asked him what was wrong. Ishmael began talking like a madman, laughing, speaking incoherently, fragmenting words, his entire body shivering intensely. Piotr went and got the Princess. But Ishmael recognized no one: he was delirious.

When the doctor arrived, he had no difficulty in diagnosing brain fever, and since he knew the story of the little poet, he couldn't prevent himself from mumbling:

"It doesn't surprise me, actually . . ."

"Is he going to die?" asked the Princess, in anguish.

"Well, yes," said the doctor, as if it were the most natural thing in the world.

He deemed it impossible to save the poor little brain of the prodigal child, who'd been exhausted by the very strength of his genius. The Princess did not protest. She felt that the untimely death of Ishmael would be beautiful, that it would end his brief, unique life in a dignified manner. Nevertheless, she had tears in her eyes, but they were noble tears, the kind that come easily when reading a Greek tragedy in which pain is as serene as antique marble.

Yet Ishmael did not die.

For six weeks, he was delirious, burned with fever, clung to the edge of his bed and the folds of the bed-curtains, his eyes rolling, full of horror, the cold sweat of death at his temples and on his hands. The tapestries in the bedroom had almost completely faded with time, turning a greenish color, which made them look like those underwater scapes at the bottom of lakes. They were decorated with hunting scenes, but the characters seemed to have a vague resemblance to sea monsters; the threadbare fabric, discolored by the dampness, blurred them all into shadowy shades of green and silver.

Ishmael, terrified, imagined they were circling around him, closing in and trying to suffocate him. At other times, he thought they were drowned cadavers (he'd seen some in the past, in the port); he would scream that they were going to carry him away, accusing the Princess of delivering him to them. Then he would fall into a deep, heavy sleep and the servants would make the sign of the Cross and walk on tiptoe, as they did in houses where someone had died.

The Baruchs sat at either side of the bed and moaned out loud in Yiddish. This dying child was the collapse of all their dreams, the end of their current prosperity. And they fought with death as if it were a kind of prey, with an obstinate stubbornness that was painful to watch.

Spring had come. Lime trees, mock orange shrubs, and acacias with pinkish clusters flourished in the gardens. A branch covered in leaves rapped at Ishmael's window, like a hand, and the smell of the lilacs was too strong, and the dust that started to rise from the town's streets was all golden. The merchants set up their stalls in the town squares, on the steps in front of entrances, on the edges of the ponds, selling strawberries and bud roses. And suddenly, with the good weather, Ishmael recovered; his fever disappeared and he was no longer delirious: he recognized his parents, the doctor, the Princess. Soon he got out of bed, taller, slimmer, his beautiful curls cut off, his cheeks translucent. He was placed on a chaise longue in front of the open window and amused himself all day long by cutting leaves off the trees with scissors, creating strange shapes.

The Princess left to go abroad; she wanted to take Ishmael with her, but the doctor said:

"This young boy needs peace and quiet. His brain has been overworked and is full of impressions that are too powerful. . . . The countryside, rest, and, especially, no intellectual work. . . . Otherwise his genius and his health will disappear, and then, he'll die . . ."

The Princess owned a country house, a day's journey from the town, that she'd left in the care of stewards; she sent the child there. He did not cry when he was separated from her, but immense anguish filled his eyes, along with a silent, profound look of terror. His tense hands clutched at her dress so fiercely that he tore off a small piece of fabric. She rushed away; he stood very still for a long time, intensely contemplating the bit of lace in

his hand. Then he threw it away with a sort of rage, and
burst out sobbing.

He left that very evening.

Ishmael had never been to the countryside. When he saw
the vast plains that were beginning to turn yellow, the
thick forests, the fields, the prairies, the pastures, he was
confused, troubled: he felt endlessly unhappy and alone.
The air was too clean and tired his lungs, the dazzling
sky hurt his eyes, and the silence terrified him. In spite of
himself, he missed the clamor of the city, the *drojkis*[6]
driving by on the sharp cobblestones, the shouts of the
merchants, the songs of the drivers, the eternal, sweet
sound of the sea.

The château was closed. Ishmael lived with the caretaker
and his wife, in a large house at the end of the estate. His

---

[6] A *drojki* is a small wagon, traditionally made of a single plank of wood
set on four wheels.—Trans.

room was on the ground floor, and trees surrounded it so closely that it was always a little dark inside, like in brushwood.

At the beginning, the fresh air made Ishmael dizzy, so he stayed in bed all day, dozing, his mind a blank, feeling nauseated, as if he were on the open seas. But then he managed to get up, go down into the garden, take walks through the countryside.

He approached nature with a sort of instinctive mistrust, hostility. He was truly a descendant of an impoverished race, weakened by books and fearful of the sun's light. Nature wounded him: he did not even find it beautiful. He was a little poet who could be moved by a muddy, dark, sloping street beneath a flickering gaslight in the morning wind, yet he could not comprehend the nobility, the appeal, of nature's great forests and fields. He avoided it; he resented the silence, the charming logic, the peacefulness with which nature cradled his feverish mind, the too-sweet torpor that linked him to it.

He wanted to compose new songs.

He took some paper and a pencil and went to a small, abandoned prairie covered in large umbels and wild grasses. And there, he confidently waited for his usual genius to appear. He knew so well how it came to him: his brain would become extremely lucid and his thoughts would take shape with striking precision, already completely full of images, everything formed and chased as if by the hands of some mysterious goldsmith.

Now, however, only a vague, craven satisfaction filled his poor, weary mind. From the tall grass rose a continuous buzzing, faint and soft, like the very song of summer; the birds were silent; a small nearby stream trickled with a clear sound.

And Ishmael quietly said three little words again and again, always the same words: "It's beautiful weather . . . it's beautiful weather . . ." with such happiness that his heart seemed to swell with peace. Beside him, a white butterfly rose up from a tuft of grass, making a zigzag pattern. Eyes wide, Ishmael watched it; the butterfly hovered, at first settling on the trembling edge of the flowers; then it took off at a dizzying speed, its little wings flapping with an endless vibration that was like the rhythm of summer itself, like a tremor, the echo of some mysterious music emerging from the depths of the earth. It flew toward Ishmael. The boy threw away his pencil and paper, and with his cheeks on fire, he let out a brief, wild, naïve cry and rushed to follow the butterfly. And from that day onward, he stopped writing.

He got up before sunrise. The garden, moist with dew, was still asleep in that unique silence before the awakening of the birds. He would walk through the woods, eating a bit of bread and the fruits he gathered for lunch. He walked for hours at a time through the brambles or dozed by the side of a path; he carved whistles out of the reeds, like the little boys in the village. Like them, he would kill the snakes that slept in the thickets. He would swim in the wide, calm river that flowed around the grounds, surrounding the Princess's domain like a band of silver.

During his walks, he discovered a thousand things that enchanted or surprised him, in particular, the birds and their different calls, and the mysterious life of the earth: ants, insects, plants, and unfamiliar berries, some bitter, some sweet. And the flowers: flowers of the forest, flowers of the fields, flowers that grew on the plains, the tall, black irises at the river's edge, the poppies among the wheat. . . . The tiniest blade of grass now aroused his passion, rooted him to the spot, captivated him for hours. He began to feel something he'd never felt before: the simple, healthy, profound joy of living, so similar to the pleasure of drinking the cool water from a well when he was thirsty, or sleeping in the sun on the warm, fragrant earth in July, or running aimlessly through the grass until he was out of breath, while the wind whipped through his disheveled hair. Never had Ishmael truly been a child: in the ghetto, he had always harbored in his heart a kind of vague anguish, an elusive desire, an overpowering sense of pride, an almost agonizing ability to fill himself with beauty and sadness. But this vigor, this simplicity of the soul, the absence of thoughts and needs, this carefree way of life now filled him as if fresh blood were flowing through him. In his mind, which had been weakened by his illness, there were now a few clear ideas: "it's beautiful weather . . . ," "it's going to rain," "I'm thirsty, let's have some fruit," "there's the cuckoo," "look, there are some blackberries . . ." And in his soul was the immense, luminous, happiness of satiated animals and plants in the warmth of summer.

One evening, however, the glory of the sun setting above the pale, calm river, the supernatural silence of the countryside and, somewhere, very far away, the song of a young farm girl bringing home her cows, the flowing sweetness of the air, the golden specks that danced on the final, slanting rays of sunshine—all these things stirred within him his former genius, which had lain dormant for so many months. But almost immediately, an insurmountable lethargy flooded his mind, a profound numbness, a sensation of emptiness that surprised him, a kind of painful weariness. He wanted to persevere. With great difficulty, he put together a verse, but then he felt pain in his head, an unbearable feeling of heaviness, and, once more, a sensation of emptiness that was almost physical. The sun, meanwhile, had set; the river was turning blue; the farm girl had stopped singing; at the edge of the woods covered in shadows, a light shone; another was lit a bit farther away. The darkness made the immense countryside seem even larger; in a corner of the land, all the lights of the village shone, and when he looked up, Ishmael saw the stars in the sky lighting up as well, one by one, like candles in the darkness of a church. So he walked more quickly toward the house, for he was hungry.

He felt that his body kept all its health and lifeblood for itself alone, without retaining even a tiny bit for his mind, which was sweetly numbed and still bruised from the terrible shock that had almost managed to destroy him forever. He had grown taller, gained some weight; his arms and legs had visible muscles and now ended in a man's hands and feet. His cheeks were pink and tanned; when he swam, he looked with astonishment at his chest, which was beginning to be covered in soft down. And his body was changing, suddenly losing its fragility, its slenderness, the exquisite delicateness of a bauble that, in the past, had so pleased the Princess. Nothing now remained of the child prodigy, but a handsome young man was growing in his place, a robust young man, like all the other young men. And he ingenuously yielded to the joy of being strong, simple, and happy.

Now summer was over, and a brief letter from the Princess announced that she would be spending the winter in Italy. Ishmael would remain in the countryside. He saw autumn come, with its heavy rain, and then, almost immediately, the first snowfall; the magical Russian winter held sway over the earth, the trees, and the river. Some days were surprisingly still and serene: pink skies the color of sugar candy above the forests, hours of silvery silence troubled only by the distant little bells on the woodsmen's sleighs. There were evenings that ended in a blaze of glory, wondrous sunsets that lit up the steppes, and glacial nights where enormous stars flickered, all tinted blue and as close as the eyes of a friend. Ishmael spent his days outside as if it were the middle of summer; he walked for miles on the plains or accompanied the farmers in their rustic sleighs, which glided along the roads with no noise apart from the eternal, melancholy little tinkling of the bells around the horses' necks.

But when the north wind blew, blasting the countryside with its gusts and snowstorms, Ishmael would take refuge inside the château. He had gotten the key to the library from the caretaker; it was a room with a low ceiling, full of books, and decorated with large black leather sofas. He would settle in an armchair next to the wood-burning stove, which hummed softly. In every alcove, there was a marble bust with serene features and dead eyes. Ishmael would read. On the windowpanes, the ice had traced marvelous forest scenes, intricate lace-work, plants and flowers as if from a dream. Nothing was comparable to the sweetness, the silence of this enclosed room where the books lived.

Ishmael read the way you become intoxicated; he would emerge from reading with his mind on fire, lost, dazed, as if he had been suddenly awakened from a dream. There were poems that he couldn't speak out loud without weeping, and others that filled him with an emotion that was almost like terror. And when he remembered his songs, they seemed so pitiful, so awkward, so inept and foolish that he felt infinitely ashamed, humiliated, and miserable. He tried to persevere, tried to imitate all those poets with their golden voices, but an immense sense of discouragement flowed through him: the words he could capture in the past as if they were docile birds now flew far away from him, became terrifying and full of hostile mystery.

All the clever rhymes and rhythms "they" played with as easily as if on some simple, dependable instrument; their ability, which created unique harmony from a simple assembling of words, a thousand times richer and more varied than music—these things crushed him, the poor thing, filled his eyes with tears of rage, impotence, and despair. He could not understand how the Princess and the Barine could have listened, without laughing, to his boorish verses, with their naïve assonance, their crude circuitousness, their simplistic images. He did not understand the charm that the spontaneous poetry of a child prodigy could have to the ears of those jaded people. Rejecting, out of disgust, the popular art that had previously inspired him without him realizing it, he slavishly forced himself to copy Pushkin, Lermontov, foreigners, the Ancients: to no avail, of course. And he fought with his rebellious rhymes like a madman who tries to reproduce melodies by Wagner using a pathetic reed pipe. Then he began reading works on criticism and doctrine, imagining, in his innocence, that poetry could be learned, like mathematics, through application and strength of will. It was a disaster. In the name of rules that made as much sense to him as Chinese, he saw that some critics condemned what others approved; he was lost in the inextricable forest of literary criticism; he completely lost his mind. Good God! So it was necessary to respond to so many objections when writing, to satisfy so many multiple and contradictory demands!

Then, to his dismay, he read scholarly books that analyzed the act of writing, all the complex cogs in the mechanism of creation, and he was like a man who, on the point of accomplishing some insignificant gesture, would have to seek out all the infinitesimal elements that make up the will to act, and he would be left dazed, distraught, facing the sheet of paper that remained obstinately blank. But when he looked up and saw the countryside stretched out before him, he would flee far away from human knowledge.

Spring arrived and the snow melted. In the neighboring town, Ishmael met a young girl his own age, the daughter of Jacob Schmul, the grocer. He was Jewish—there were a lot of Jews in the small town—and they went about their buying and selling rather freely. The daughter was called Rachel. She wore the brown dress and black smock of a schoolgirl, and on either side of her face she had long red curls, as coarse as a stallion's tail. She would wait for Ishmael on the rough roads, where the carriages would get stuck in the mud. He would take her hand and guide her along the edges of the ditches that were lined with melted snow, as brown and thick as pastry crust, until they reached the grocer's, which was the first house in the village. They chatted with her father in Yiddish, the husky, melodious language Ishmael had never forgotten. Schmul left Rachel and Ishmael alone without fear: the boy was Jewish, and Schmul was only afraid of the "goys," the officers and gentlemen who came to drink in the nearby inns on Saturday nights. They alone would dishonor Jewish girls with neither fear nor remorse.

And he was not wrong. The romance between Rachel and Ishmael was innocent during the time when the snow was melting. In the springtime, however, that changed: they took long walks in the prairies and wandered through the woods. Ishmael was turning fifteen, and the provocative scent of Rachel's red hair reminded him of the women who had taught him, when still a child, how to make love.

They walked together through the forests, along the
steppes. They stole kisses. And then, one beautiful June
morning that smelled of strawberries, he took her among
the branches of a birch tree that had fallen and lay in a
clearing. And throughout the entire summer, they played
at being in love, the way they had played at being "pirates."
It truly seemed that nature—obstinate, stubborn nature—
wanted, at all costs, to have Ishmael relive the childhood
that his friends from the port and the caresses of the beautiful ladies had stolen from him. But the late arrival of his
early youth came with the complications and troubles of
everything that does not happen when it is supposed to.

One day—it was in the month of October, when in Russia
there are extended stretches of fog, sudden cold spells,
long, early downpours—Ishmael had just left Rachel in
the shed, where they had spent two hours together. He
was walking up to the front of the house when he saw, to
his great astonishment, the wife of the caretaker, who had
been looking for him.

"Hurry up, Ishmael," she shouted, "someone's waiting
for you."

Ishmael went completely pale and stopped, rooted to the spot with surprise; suddenly, his entire past struck him in the face, like a whiff of perfume. . . . "Someone" . . . who could that be if not the Princess? His forgotten love for her filled his heart once more. He could picture her imperious face, her black dress, the hard diamond that had wounded his cheek. . . . He rushed into the entrance hall, pushing past the smiling woman. But it was not the Princess. It was his father who was waiting for him, sitting with the caretaker; they were drinking large cups of tea. His father . . . older, thinner, more bent over; a small American-style mustache had replaced the *payos* of the past. His initial disappointment gone, Ishmael leapt to hug his father, feeling true joy; his father looked at him for a long time with his small, searching eyes.

"You've gotten so big," he finally said, nodding, as if scolding him. "You've gotten so big . . ."

Ishmael asked him about his health, and how his mother was, his life, business; his father replied briefly, still staring at his son with an expression of sadness.

"You've had your curls cut off?" he asked.

"Well, Father, I'm fifteen," Ishmael protested with a laugh.

"I know . . ." his father replied with a small, bittersweet smile. "I know . . . too bad . . ." Then he asked harshly, "Are you working?"

"Working at what?" asked Ishmael, surprised. "I have no teachers."

His father made a vague gesture. "Hmm . . . you know very well what I mean . . . not schoolwork, but your songs, your poetry?"

Ishmael lowered his gaze as if he felt guilty. Baruch shook his head without saying a word. He stared in obvious displeasure at this tall, strong adolescent with his awkward gestures and ordinary features, so different from the child he had known.

"I hope I haven't come too late," he finally said, pursing his lips.

Ishmael gave his father the fearful look of a young boy caught doing something bad.

"We're leaving here tomorrow," Baruch continued. "I've come to get you. You're completely well now, I think . . ." he added with the same tone of inexplicable hostility.

"Yes, yes," Ishmael muttered, "perhaps . . ." Then he asked, in a voice choked with emotion, "Is the Princess asking me to come back?"

Baruch made a very terrible face that was meant to be a smile.

"The Princess . . . she doesn't think about you much any-more, my boy. The Princess . . . she brought two big dogs back from Italy, a monkey, and a kind of worthless person who plays the mandolin badly, or the violin, I don't know . . ."

He hesitated for a moment, then concluded: "So, I thought . . . I came to get you. We have to refresh the Princess's memory. She's a woman, a great lady, but forgetful . . ."

That night, for the first time in eighteen months, Ishmael could not sleep. He turned over and over in his bed but could not rid his heavy heart of its vague anguish. And always the same feeling of crushing shame wounded him, though he was unable to understand the dark reason for it.

The next morning, he said his good-byes to Rachel in the shed. She had been waiting for him, as serene and sweet as ever. When she saw him, she had a little mocking smile on her face, along with the somewhat insulted look in her eyes that he knew well, and that always intimidated him a little. He coldly announced that he was leaving; she suddenly seemed so distant. He was very surprised and rather annoyed when she began to cry. "I'll come back," he told her, looking down, embarrassed. Then he kissed her and rushed off, completely astonished, as any young man would be, by the unexpected expression of defeat and despair in her eyes.

On the train, Ishmael's father explained that he had made disastrous speculations on the last wheat harvest. To be honest, he said, he owed a substantial amount of

money—five thousand rubles—to Rabinovitch, the most
callous of moneylenders. "Your grandfather," he added,
"is an angel sent from Heaven compared to him."
Naturally, he'd gone to speak to the Princess, but she had
quickly sent him on his way. But as she had always
spoiled and adored her little poet, Baruch was certain that
she would easily grant Ishmael such a mere bagatelle. He
said this over and over again to Ishmael, who remained
silent and motionless. Yet Baruch was filled with inexplicable anxiety: of course the Princess would have given
anything to the Ishmael of the past, but to this big, awkward boy? And his father continued to question him
harshly about his songs, asking him if he had brought
any to show to the Princess, virtually demanding that
he compose some right then and there, in front of him,
without noticing the terrified, dazed look on the poor
boy's face.

Finally, Baruch fell asleep in his corner, and Ishmael
bravely got to work. The train kept moving with an
unnerving, rumbling sound. The child, his mind a blank,
tried in vain to gather together ideas, words, stubborn
rhymes. Nothing . . . he could find nothing . . . and tears

began to fill his eyes; impotent rage stung his heart. Then he too fell asleep, completely exhausted.

The next day, Baruch took him to see the Princess. Ishmael recognized at once the blue boudoir, the deep armchair, the cushion where he had so often knelt at the Princess's feet. However, he stood there speechless, paralyzed by some atrocious shyness. All this luxury, which had neither surprised nor troubled him when he was simply an unhappy, down-and-out little vagabond, now left him breathless, prevented him from speaking, moving, thinking. He had lost the ephemeral kingdom of childhood. In the past, the richness of his internal vision had obscured the visible world to him. In the past, he had accepted all of it—the carpets, the perfumes, the imperious beauty of this woman—calmly and effortlessly. In the past, he had been a child prodigy; now he was nothing more than a boy who was as gauche and stupid as any other. The Princess looked at him with her cold eyes. Two white dogs slept on the ground beside her. She herself was dressed in white. Ishmael was shaking from head to toe; a kind of fog floated in front of him: all he could see through that mist, in painful detail, were his own hands,

red, too big, with their bitten nails, clasping each other
nervously. The Princess frowned. Such a shame! So this
is what that wondrous child had become when he grew
up? A strong, rugged adolescent with neither beauty nor
genius. Nevertheless, she tried to get him to speak.

"Well, Ishmael, don't you recognize me? Am I frightening
you? Why won't you say anything? Let's see, have you com-
posed any new songs in these past months? Tell me, speak."

His temples throbbing, his throat dry, he mumbled, "Yes,
Madame."

"Well then, let me hear them."

He stood silent, in despair.

She asked him a few more questions, trying to soften
her biting voice. But he lowered his head even more and
simply murmured, "Yes, Madame," and "No, Madame,"
sounding stupid, his lips frozen in anguish.

Irritated, she finally sent him away.

Wunderkind . . . that's what they had found to hurt
him . . . "child prodigy." . . . Oh! The irony of that name! They
didn't treat him badly, didn't scold him; they simply stared
at him with harsh, mocking eyes while mumbling under
their breath in a kind of bastardized German and Yiddish:
Wunderkind. His father, his mother, his grandfather, and
the host of Jews who had been so proud of this genius who
had miraculously appeared in their midst—they all said the
same thing, with scorn and anger, "*Wunderkind,* sure,
Wunderkind," until Ishmael, who was sweet and incapable
of evil, felt his fingers tingling and had red rages that made
him want to kill them all. Was it his fault, after all? It was
too monstrously unfair, in the end, to demand that he be a
genius! "Work, read!" all those ignorant, moronic people
told him, over and over again. And he did work, the poor
boy, with no order, no method; he spent entire nights leaning over the table, his head heavy enough to burst. He
wrote, then crossed out the awful verses, which he would
immediately tear up, paralyzed by the idea that he would
have to give them to the Princess.

He lived at home with his parents now, but not in the
beautiful apartment in the city, which had become too

expensive for them ever since the Princess's generosity had ended; now they lived with Salomon, Baruch's father-in-law, in the small shop in the ghetto. All night long, Ishmael could hear the old man snoring through the thin walls; the oil lamp gave off smoke that made him cough. He thought with despair about the countryside and his carefree life there; then he cursed it, seeing in it—and not without good reason, perhaps—the loss of his genius, for he was trying to understand.

Why had the songs that in the past had been so sponta-neously born on his lips suddenly disappeared? Was it because of his illness? Or, on the contrary, was it because he had regained his good health, a normal life? Had his genius been a kind of deadly flower, blossoming only because his life had been violent, excessive, corrupt? Did he need the chaotic atmosphere of the inns of the port, the excitement of wine and caresses for that flower to flour-ish? Alas! It was quite simply because he was entering the difficult age of adolescence, when his body had sud-denly become the body of a man, which robbed his intelli-gence of its lifeblood, and because well-meaning nature, while wishing him to live, brought a halt, in its wisdom, to the divine source of his genius. But no one told him all this; no one gave him hope that he would again recover his charming, fatal gift later on, when he became a man. No one was there to whisper to him, "Wait, have hope . . ." They all leaned over him, around him, clinging to him, like people who wish to force open a flower with their sacrilegious fingers. And in the desolate silence of the night, he would sob, feeling so weak, so insignificant, tortured in a cowardly, unjust way. He thought of the Princess as if she were some terrible god; he remembered the past, when he had been held in her arms, feeling the warmth of her breasts, without fear. Why didn't she love him anymore? He was madly jealous of the big white dogs . . . why wouldn't she let him take their place, at her feet? Then he would sob even more, with a feeling of humiliation that was more agonizing than any physical pain. Those dogs were so beautiful . . .

ॐ

For the tenth time that month, Baruch had dragged Ishmael to see the Princess, and once again, faced with all her questions, the boy had responded with idiotic silence, happy to simply look at her with the suffering eyes of a dog you wanted to drown.

"What can I say? We made a mistake," she said indifferently. "Get him an apprenticeship; that's all. . . . I'll pay for it," she added. "My secretary will give you the money." And as she found this old, obsequious Jew and his ridiculous child truly boring, she added: "There's no point in coming back."

"Lazy, stupid, little runt!" his father grumbled, inconsolable.

The money wasn't enough for him. To have dreamed of being the father of a famous poet and instead finding himself with a future shoemaker or secondhand clothes dealer! And besides, who would take him on as an apprentice, at fifteen, when he was used to such a comfortable, luxurious way of life?

He moaned when he saw his wife and father-in-law, calling for the greatest of Jewish curses to befall the Princess, and without sparing the child either, who had so inexplicably duped them.

Finally, a month later, he was able to obtain a place for Ishmael with one of his cousins, a tailor at the port.

For three weeks, the poor boy, dazed and mistreated, had to learn how to sew in a dark, dingy room that smelled of garlic and oil.

An immense sadness crushed him, a horrible feeling of degradation, a vain and sterile revolt against life, people, God . . .

One winter night, instead of going home, he wandered around the port. He hesitated a moment at the crossroads, then, without erring, took the road he was looking for from among all the muddy little back alleys: instinctively, he headed toward the Bout-du-Quai *traktir*. The sound of the sea striking the walls of the jetty guided him. Finally, he stopped. He recognized the entrance, with its broken-down steps, and the red light, a little farther away, opposite the brothel.

Someone was playing the harmonica, pulling thin, reedy sounds from it, and drunken voices joined in to sing a sad, obscene refrain. Ishmael went inside; nothing had changed. He could see everything as if he had left the day before: the tables covered in dirty cloths, the lamp beneath the icon in the corner, the samovar, the bottles standing in a row along the wall. But the men were no longer the same, nor the women: the men he remembered had either gone away or were dead; the women, probably to a hospital or a brothel.

Ishmael shuddered: opposite him, a man was drinking. It was the Barine. His fur hat pulled down to his eyes, he was holding a glass of vodka in his shaking hand. He had changed, aged. His poorly shaven chin made him look unkempt. Ishmael could also see that his clothes were old, patched up.

Ishmael walked over to him. "Hello. Do you recognize me?"

"Is it you, boy!"

A vague smiled appeared on the Barine's impassive face. He pointed to a seat opposite him. "Sit down there. . . . Do you want something to drink?"

He spoke with difficulty, and his words seemed to get mud-
dled in his mouth, as if he had lost the ability to use human
language. The boy sat down, shyly clutching his overalls
with both hands. Because he was bent over his painstaking
work all day long, he had pins and needles in his hands,
sharp pains in his neck, stinging eyes. He drank a large
glass of vodka in one gulp; it felt as if fire were suddenly
rushing through his veins. Yet he remained silent,
strangely moved by the way the Barine looked. His eyes, all
red and swollen, especially hypnotized him.

"You don't live . . . there . . . anymore?" asked the Barine.

"No," replied Ishmael, lowering his head. Then he got up
the courage to ask:

"What about you . . . ? The Princess?"

The Barine wiped his forehead with his unsteady hand.
"As you can see."

They drank, sinking deeper and deeper into a kind
of morose delirium; they could hear their hearts

beating; the visible world was shrouded in fog and darkness.

A vague idea came into Ishmael's mind. He had to go home . . . the next day . . . get up early . . . work. He made a move to stand up, then fell heavily back onto his seat.

"Never mind, come on," the Barine told him. "*This* is the only thing that's good."

"I'm so miserable," muttered Ishmael, "so miserable . . ."

Bitter tears fell down his cheeks; he wiped them away with the back of his sleeve, which was splattered with alcohol.

The Barine shrugged. "Miserable . . . look at me. A king, I was more than a king. Oh! My poems . . . my beautiful poems. Why did God give me such genius only to take it away so soon? Don't think I'm blaspheming. God, you see, is formidable, and I would say nothing against His glory. I only ask, in despairing humility, 'All-powerful God, why have you taken away what You had given me? Did I ever use it for anything but to glorify Your works and Your being? I worked hard, Lord, so why take away the tool from my hands?'"

He raised his shaking hands to the heavens, then placed them on Ishmael's head.

"Little one, little one, do you understand? Do you? Here, in my mind, in my heart, there are beautiful poems, there is poetry . . . I can feel it beating within me like the wings of birds. Here, do you see? And I can't write. When I try to capture my birds, they fly away . . . far, far away. You won't tell anyone, will you? Before, they also flew away. Then I captured them again, in wine or on *her* mouth. But now when I drink, it's my head, my poor head that hurts so much, I feel it will burst, and you'd think that evil demons were taunting me: 'Go on, try, just try a bit more . . . again, just try a tiny bit more.' Nothing, nothing. Listen, I'm going to tell you something, but you can't tell anyone else. Maybe . . . I don't dare say it out loud, but maybe they're dead, my wondrous birds; maybe they're no more than a little pile of feathers, a very tiny heap of dead feathers. Lord, oh Lord, why have you taken away my gift?"

Ishmael's hand was on the table; the Barine absentmindedly stroked it.

"She sent me away" he said. "But I loved her . . . I cried.
She looked at me and laughed. Why? Tell me why? Was it
my fault? Was it my fault that I couldn't write anymore?
Yet I still love her. . . . Little one, little one, what have we
done to the good Lord to be so severely punished?"

Then he fell silent and, once again, drank some more. In
his eyes was a kind of immense stupor.

The innkeeper came over to tell them that he was closing
up. They went outside, into the cold night.

They walked, steadying themselves by holding on to the
houses. On the ground, they saw some men leaning over
a blackish mass. It was a dead horse; his long teeth
gleamed faintly in the darkness.

"If I still knew how to write," said the Barine, "I'd tell the
story of a horse I once had. He was beautiful. Boïar was
his name, and he truly looked like the lord of the beasts. I

remember his fine legs, which trembled after a ride, damp with sweat. He grew old, very old. I didn't love him anymore. He was well cared for, it's true, but I no longer felt proud of him in my heart. His eyes followed me, and seemed full of feelings. I understand now. He was asking me, 'Why? But it's not my fault. I would love to be young and handsome again. You're ashamed of me, but I still love you.' I killed him, little one. Death alone can save us. If only we could die!"

"We can always die," said Ishmael.

An immense light rose from within him, a great sense of comfort.

"But I'm afraid," said the Barine, hunching over.

The next day, they found Ishmael hanging in the shed. His body was swaying above a pile of cut logs. He had given himself death with simplicity, a humble death, with no fanfare, in a dark corner, among the cobwebs.

His parents mourned him for a long time. After all, he had been a good, docile child, even intelligent. Why had he taken his own life? Children are strange and cruel. Now they would be alone in their old age.

Ishmael was buried in the Jewish cemetery among the very old graves, which were slowly crumbling. No one took care of them, for the cemetery was far from the town and the roads were bad, full of rough patches because of the snow.

The following spring, his parents went to visit him. On the gravestone, they found a bouquet of roses, still very fresh. They recognized the homage of the Princess. They threw the flowers far away, for Jewish law prohibits giving flowers to the dead, who are only putrefaction. His father, his soul full of anger and outrage, stamped on the roses for a long time. But before leaving, according to the rite, they placed a handful of pebbles onto their son's grave.

Then they left.

And this is how Ishmael Baruch, the prodigal child, lived and died.

ACKNOWLEDGMENTS

My gratitude goes to my husband, Peter Smith, for his endless patience and encouragement. Many thanks as well to Patricia Freestone, Philippe Savary, and Dr. Paul Micio for their help, and to Kales Press for giving me the opportunity to translate this book.

Sandra Smith